The Magic of Christmas
A Treasury of Holiday Stories
LITTLE TIGER PRESS
An imprint of Magi Publications
1 The Coda Centre, 189 Munster Road,
London SW6 6AW
www.littletigerpress.com

First published in Great Britain 2005
This volume copyright © Magi Publications 2011
Cover illustration copyright © Jane Chapman 2005
All rights reserved

Printed in China • LTP/1400/0333/0911
ISBN 978-1-84895-464-9
2 4 6 8 10 9 7 5 3 1

I've Seen Santa!
David Bedford
Illustrated by Tim Warnes
First published in Great Britain 2005
by Little Tiger Press,
an imprint of Magi Publications
Text copyright © David Bedford 2005
Illustrations copyright © Tim Warnes 2005

Careful, Santa!
Julie Sykes
Illustrated by Tim Warnes
First published in Great Britain 2002
by Little Tiger Press,
an imprint of Magi Publications
Text copyright © Julie Sykes 2002
Illustrations copyright © Tim Warnes 2002

Bless You, Santa!
Julie Sykes
Illustrated by Tim Warnes
First published in Great Britain 2004
by Little Tiger Press,
an imprint of Magi Publications
Text copyright © Julie Sykes 2004
Illustrations copyright © Tim Warnes 2004

The Gift of Christmas
Christine Leeson
Illustrated by Gaby Hansen
First published in Great Britain 2000
by Little Tiger Press,
an imprint of Magi Publications
Text copyright © Christine Leeson 2000
Illustrations copyright © Gaby Hansen 2000

The Magic of Christmas

A Treasury of Holiday Stories

Merry Christmas

BLESS YOU, SANTA!

by Julie Sykes
illustrated by Tim Warnes

THE GIFT
OF CHRISTMAS

by Christine Leeson
illustrated by Gaby Hansen

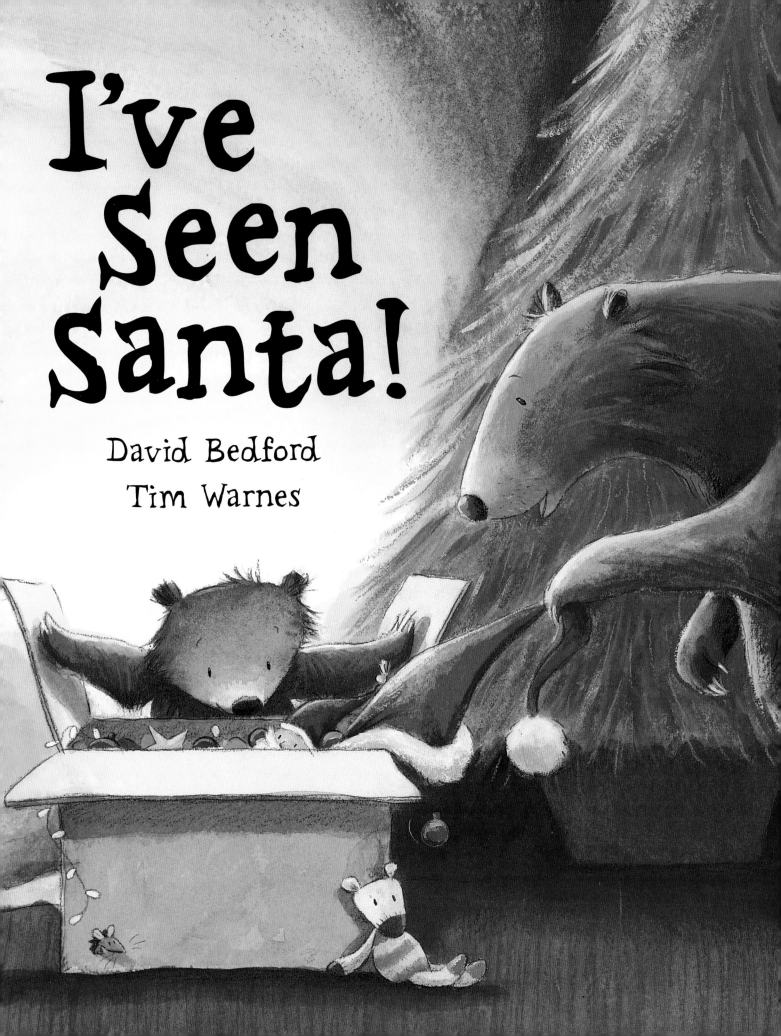

I've Seen Santa!

David Bedford

Tim Warnes

It was Christmas Eve,
and Little Bear was looking
forward to seeing Santa.
  "Is Santa as big as you?"
he asked Big Bear.

"Nearly," said Big Bear, proudly.

"Oh," said Little Bear, looking worried.

"Will Santa fit down our chimney, then?"

"Of course he will!" said Big Bear. "I'll show you."

Big Bear went outside and climbed into

the chimney . . .

CRASH!

"See?" said Big Bear, from a cloud of soot.
"Santa will get in, no problem!"

"Santa won't come if he sees this mess!"
said Mommy Bear.
"We'll help clean up," said Little Bear.

"Does Santa visit bears
all over the world?"
said Little Bear.
    "Yes," said Big Bear.
"He goes to every
    house."

"Hmm," said Little Bear. "He might not have time to come here, and then I won't have any presents."

"Don't worry," said Mommy Bear. "Santa will come just as soon as you go to sleep."

15

Little Bear didn't want to go to sleep.
He wanted to see Santa. He listened to
Mommy Bear and Big Bear going to bed.
And then . . . GLUG, GLUG, GLUG, GLUG!

What was that noise?
Someone was downstairs!

Someone big was sitting
by the fireplace.
"Yes!" whispered Little Bear.
"It's Santa! I've seen Santa!"
Little Bear tiptoed up and saw . . .

Big Bear!

"That's Santa's milk!" said Little Bear.

"I only wanted a sip," said Big Bear, "before I go to sleep." He took Little Bear's hand. "Come on, Little Bear. Let's go to bed."

Little Bear tried to stay awake, but he soon began to doze.

Then a loud noise downstairs woke him up.

MUNCH! MUNCH! MUNCH! MUNCH!

Someone big was
standing by the
Christmas tree.
This time it had to be . . .

Big Bear again!

"You're eating Santa's blueberry pies now!" said Little Bear.

"I was hungry," said Big Bear.

"If Santa's as greedy as you," said Mommy Bear, coming downstairs, "he really WILL be too big to fit down the chimney! Now go to bed and go to sleep— both of you!"

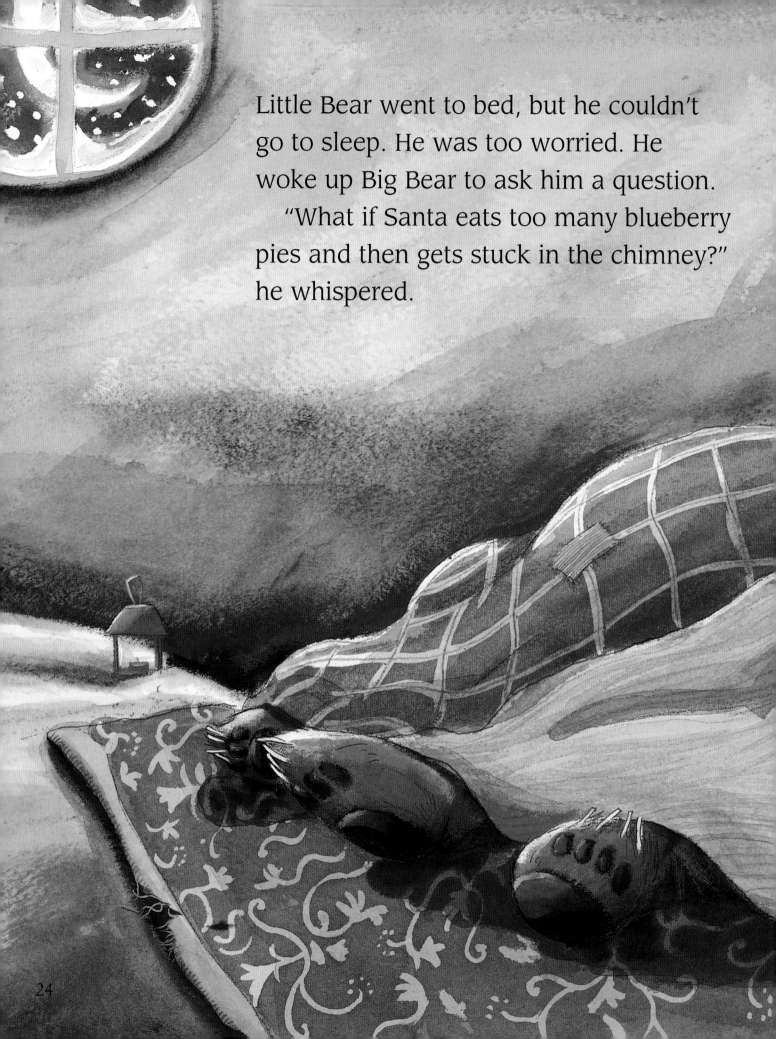

Little Bear went to bed, but he couldn't go to sleep. He was too worried. He woke up Big Bear to ask him a question.

"What if Santa eats too many blueberry pies and then gets stuck in the chimney?" he whispered.

"Hmm," said Big Bear.

"Let's keep watch to make sure he's OK," said Little Bear. "We can hide so he won't see us."

"Shhh!" whispered Little Bear
from their hiding place.
"I can hear something.
  It MUST be Santa this time!"

Someone was putting
presents in their stockings!
Big Bear turned on his
flashlight to see . . .

27

Mommy Bear!

"What are YOU doing?" said Big Bear.
"I'm giving you both a present from me,"
said Mommy Bear. "What are YOU doing?"
"We're not going to bed," said Big Bear.
"We're going to see Santa!"
squealed Little Bear.

Mommy Bear laughed.
"Make room for me,
then," she said. "We'll
ALL see Santa."

29

Little Bear, Big Bear, and
Mommy Bear stayed downstairs
all through the night.

But they never did see Santa . . .

. . . even though
Santa saw them!

Careful, Santa!

North Pole

Julie Sykes
Tim Warnes

It was Christmas Eve, and
Santa was loading presents
onto his sleigh. Santa's little
mouse was helping, too.

WHOOSH!

A gust of wind blew Santa's
beard straight in his face.
"Ho, ho, ho!" he chuckled.
"I can't see what I'm doing!"
"Careful, Santa!" warned
Santa's cat. "Don't lose
that bag of presents."

"That would be terrible!"
Santa agreed, as he carefully
placed the bag on the sleigh.

Santa helped his little mouse climb aboard
the sleigh. "Hold on tight!" he boomed.
"We're off!"
    It was a wild and windy night.
    "Oh, my!" shouted Santa, as the sleigh
rocked this way and that.
    Suddenly, the bag of presents began to move.
    "Careful, Santa!" called Santa's little mouse.
"Watch those presents!"

But Santa wasn't quick enough. The bag of presents
slid across the sleigh and toppled overboard.
"Stop!" cried Santa in alarm. "Down, reindeer, down!
I've lost all the presents!"

The reindeer struggled
against the wind . . .

. . . and landed as gently as they could.
"Careful, Santa!" they shouted, but it
was too late . . .
"WHOOPS!" cried Santa, landing on
his bottom.

Santa scrambled to his feet.
The presents were scattered far and
wide, and he hurried to pick them up.
He didn't notice the frozen pond.

"Whee!" cried Santa, as he slid across
the ice toward the duck house.

"Careful, Santa!" quacked the ducks.
"You nearly squashed us."
    "How awful," said Santa as he picked
up the presents. "Sorry about that.
Has anyone seen my present bag?"

"Here it is!" chattered
a squirrel from high
in a tree.
   Santa bravely
climbed up, but before
he knew it, he was
stuck in the branches.
"Oh, help!" he cried.

48

"Careful, Santa!"
called the squirrel.
  "I am trying to
be careful," said Santa,
as he struggled to get free.
  Very slowly, Santa climbed
back down, dropping
some presents as he went.

At the playground, a few presents were lying under the swings. Santa put them into his bag, then he spotted some more on the slide.

"Whoosh!" cried Santa, as he zoomed down the slide.

"Careful, Santa, you're going too fast!" warned Santa's cat.

"Eek! I can't stop!" said Santa, as he slid toward a snowman.

"Sorry, snowman, I didn't mean to bump you," Santa
said, as he dusted himself off and popped the last of
the presents into his bag.

"That's it!" he boomed. "It's time to
deliver these presents. Ready, mouse?"
But where was Santa's mouse?
Santa couldn't see her anywhere.
"Oh, dear!" he cried. "First I lose
my bag of presents, and now
I've lost my little mouse.
This is horrible."

The ducks, the squirrel, and Santa's cat all
crowded around.

"Don't worry, Santa!" they chattered. "She
can't be very far. We'll help you look for her."

Everyone looked for Santa's mouse. She wasn't in the duck house. She wasn't near the slide or behind the snowman.

Just then, Santa heard a familiar squeak. He shined his flashlight up . . .

. . . and there was his mouse, hanging from a branch in a tree.
"Careful!" warned Santa. "It's far too windy to play up there.
That branch doesn't look too safe to me."

But the mouse wasn't playing. "I'm stuck," she squeaked. "Please get me down!" Quickly, Santa took off his jacket and spread it out on the ground. Everyone gathered around and held the coat like a trampoline. "Hold on tight, everyone, and don't let go!" said Santa.

"Ready, mouse?
One, two, three . . .

JUMP!"

Mouse jumped and, with a bounce and a plop,
she landed safely on Santa's coat.
"Hooray!" cheered Santa. "Thank you, everyone."

It was time to go. Santa and his mouse hurried to their sleigh.

"Reindeer, up, up, and away!" cried Santa. *Whoosh!* blew the wind.

"Careful, Santa," called everyone,
as the sleigh rocked this way and that.
"Look after that mouse, and HOLD
ON TIGHT TO THOSE PRESENTS!"

Bless You, Santa!

Julie Sykes   Tim Warnes

It was almost Christmas, and Santa was up
very early one day.

"Jingle bells, jingle bells," he sang to himself.
"Breakfast first and then to work."

He made some toast and took out the
jam and butter. As he was pouring some
cereal, though, his nose began to tickle.

"Aah, aah, aah . . ."

"Achoooo!"

he roared. His sneeze blew the cereal all over the place!

"Bless you, Santa," said Santa's cat, shaking cereal out of her tail. "That's a nasty cold."

"Oh, no!" said Santa in alarm. "It can't be. It's nearly Christmas. I don't have time for a cold."

After breakfast Santa rushed to his workshop
and went to work on the unfinished toys. Happily
he sang as he painted a robot. But Santa's sneezes
were growing larger and louder.

"Aah, aah, aah…"

71

"Achoooo!"

"Bless you, Santa," squeaked
Santa's little mouse, gathering the beads
his sneezes had scattered across the table.

"Bless you, Santa," said Santa's cat, chasing paper stars as they fluttered around. "You sound awful. Go and sit by the fire."

"I feel awful!" said Santa. "But I can't rest yet. It's too close to Christmas. I have to finish these toys or there will be no presents for all the . . . *aah, aah, aah . . .*"

"Achoooo!"

Santa sneezed so hard that he slipped and landed in a pile of balls.

Down the balls tumbled, bouncing off Santa and bouncing around the room. They crashed into cars, they pushed over paint cans, they toppled the teddy bears, and they ruined the rockets.

"Achoooo!"

"Just look at this mess!"
cried Santa. "I'll never be ready
in time for Christmas."

"Go to bed, Santa," ordered Santa's little mouse. "You're not well. Your nose is so red the reindeer could use it to guide your sleigh. We'll clean up this mess and get everything ready for Christmas."

77

So Santa's mouse put Santa to bed with
a mug of hot tea and a little medicine
to help his cold.
  Santa snuggled into the blanket.
He sneezed.

"A c h o o o o !"

He sniffled . . .

And finally he snored.

sssh!

z z z Z Z Z Z Z Z Z z z z z z z z z z z z

Meanwhile, back in the workshop,
Santa's friends worked as hard as they
could. They mopped.

They mended.

They glued.

They snipped, they stuck, and they wrapped.
Faster and faster they worked until every
single present was finished. Then sleepily
they went to bed.

The next evening, as the sun set, the animals waited with a sleigh piled high with toys.

"But where is Santa?" asked Santa's cat. "I hope he's better."

"Who's going to drive the sleigh and deliver all the presents?" asked the reindeer.

"Listen," said Santa's cat. "Can you hear something?"

The animals listened.

"It's Santa!" squeaked Santa's little mouse. "Are you better, Santa? Can you deliver the presents?"

Santa wrinkled his nose. *"Aah, aah, aah . . ."*

"Ho, ho, ho!" chuckled Santa loudly.

"Only joking! I feel much better. Bless you, everyone. You did a great job! Thanks to you I will get these presents delivered in time for Christmas morning."
Santa climbed aboard his sleigh.
"Reindeer, up, up, and away!" he shouted.

It was a busy night as Santa flew
around the world delivering presents.

86

When at last Santa landed back at the
North Pole, the sun was rising. But he
hadn't finished yet.

"These presents are for you," said Santa.

"Presents for us!" squeaked Santa's cat.
"Th . . . th . . . thaa . . ."

"Achooo o!"

Santa's cat sneezed so hard that a pile of snow fell off the trees and buried everyone. "Bless you!" laughed Santa. "And Merry Christmas to you, too!"

89

THE GIFT OF
CHRISTMAS

CHRISTINE LEESON

GABY HANSEN

It was Molly Mouse's first Christmas. The sky was streaked with pink and gold, and there was a tingle in the air.

Through the window of a house something was shining and glittering into the night.

"What is that, Mom?" asked Molly.

"It's a Christmas tree," said her mother. "People cover it with shiny balls, lights, and stars."

"I wish *we* had a Christmas tree," sighed Molly.

"Why don't you go into the woods to find one?" said her mother. "You could make it look just as nice as that tree in the window."

Molly thought this was a great idea. She called her brothers and sisters together, and off they all scampered.

On the way to the woods, they came to a barn. The mice rummaged through it, looking for something to add to their tree. Under a big pile of hay, Molly found a doll.

"This is like the doll on the top of the Christmas tree in the window," she said. "It will be just right for our tree."

But the doll belonged to someone else.

"Grr!" said the old farm dog. "That's mine!"

"Don't chase us!" cried Molly. "I only thought
the doll would look nice on our Christmas tree."

The old dog yawned. It was true that sometimes
he chased mice. But because it was Christmas,
or because he remembered the Christmas tree
in the farmhouse and how he used to play
with the children there, he said the mice
could borrow the doll.

The mice left the barn and walked across
the barnyard, carrying the doll. They came to
the edge of the woods.

"Hey," Molly shouted. "I see something else
we can put on our Christmas tree!"

It was a gold ribbon, hanging from a branch
of an oak tree. Molly scampered up the trunk,
took hold of the ribbon, and pulled.

But the ribbon belonged to a magpie.
She had taken it to line her nest.
    "Please don't be angry," said Molly.
"I only wanted the gold ribbon for
our Christmas tree."

Usually the magpie chased mice. But because
it was Christmas, or because she had also been
admiring the Christmas tree in the window, she
let go of the other end of the ribbon. Molly took
the ribbon thankfully.

In the distance Molly saw some shiny round things
lying on the ground. They were like the shiny balls
on the Christmas tree in the window.

"Exactly what we want!" cried Molly, running
to pick one of them up. "Now we have a doll, a
gold ribbon, and a shiny ball!"

But those shiny balls belonged to a fox. "Those are my crab apples," he barked. "I'm saving them for the cold days ahead."

"We only thought one would look good on our Christmas tree," said Molly, trembling.

The fox sniffed. He chased mice most of the time. But because it was Christmas, or because he had never seen a Christmas tree before, he went back into the woods. Molly picked up a shiny crab apple and carried it away.

Twilight was falling as the mice went deeper into
the woods. There, in the middle of a bramble bush,
they could see a shining star and a dozen tiny lights
glittering green and gold.

"Stars for our tree!" shouted Molly. "Let me
get them." But when Molly reached into the bush,
she found not stars . . .

. . . but a collar, belonging to an angry mother cat.
She had her kittens with her and their three pairs
of eyes shone in the dark.

"Oh, no!" gulped Molly. "I only wanted something
sparkly for our Christmas tree."

The cat pricked her ears. She always chased mice.
But because it was Christmas, or because she
remembered the Christmas tree in the cozy home where
she'd been a kitten, the mother cat slipped off her collar.
She let the mice have it for their tree.

At last, in a clearing in the deepest
part of the woods, the mice found
a large evergreen tree.
  "Our Christmas tree!"
cried Molly. They hung the
doll, the ribbon, the crab apple,
and the cat's collar on the
tree's branches.

"Oh," said Molly when they had finished. "It doesn't look at all like the tree I saw in the window." Sadly, the mice turned away.

Disappointed, they walked all the way back home and went straight to bed.

In the middle of the night, the mother mouse woke up Molly and her brothers and sisters. "Come with me," she whispered. "I have something to show you."

The mice scurried along behind their mother, past the farm and into the woods. Other animals hurried on ahead of them, into the deepest part of the woods.

At last, the mice reached the clearing
where Molly's Christmas tree was.

Molly stood completely still. Her eyes
grew large and round.

"Oh, look at that!" she cried.

During the night, the animals had all added decorations to the Christmas tree. The frost had come and touched everything with glitter. The little tree sparkled, and even the stars in the sky seemed to be caught in its branches, with the biggest and brightest star right at the very top.

"Our Christmas tree is even better than the one in the window," whispered Molly happily.

And because it was Christmas, all the animals from the woods sat quietly around the tree, at peace with each other.